PENNY GOES TO RHODESIA

ELSIE MILLIGAN

D1580162

LONDON
PICKERING & INGLIS LTD.

PICKERING & INGLIS LTD.

29 LUDGATE HILL, LONDON, E.C.4

26 BOTHWELL STREET, GLASGOW, C.2

Home Evangel Books Ltd., 25 Hobson Avenue, Toronto, 16

First published –   1960
Reprinted   –   –   1968

Printed in Great Britain

CONTENTS

CHAPTER I

GOODBYE, GAME RESERVE

IT was with great reluctance that Penny and Billy and Glenny left the Game Reserve where they had had such an exciting time. When they found themselves outside of the gates at Malopene, they felt quite sad.

"May Glenny come in our car with us, Mummy?" asked Penny.

"Certainly, if her Mummy says she may."

Permission being given, Glenny got into the Dawson's car, sitting in the back with Penny and Billy, and Glenny's parents, Dr. and Mrs. Mason followed in their own car.

As they drove off on the road which would eventually join the great North road leading up to Rhodesia, Mrs. Dawson said:

"It will be funny now not to have to peer out of the car windows looking for wild animals. We shall be doing it from force of habit, I expect."

"Oh, but you may still see some animals, especially elephants," said Mr. Dawson, "I understand that quite a few of them stray out of the Reserve from time to time on to neighbouring farms, and are sometimes seen on the roads."

"Why, isn't there a fence to keep them in?" asked Glenny.

"No," said Mr. Dawson, "there is no fence round the Reserve, only round the camps where people sleep at night."

"Then how do the animals know to stay inside the Game Reserve?" asked Penny.

"Well, I guess they know pretty well where they are safe. But elephants are great travellers and do go outside sometimes, and even lions have been known to wander on to bordering farms, and then, of course, they are liable to be shot."

"Oh, dear!" said Penny in distress, "the poor lions, I hope no-one shoots those ones we saw."

"No, those were well inside the Park," said Mummy, "but I must say I am surprised to hear that the Reserve is not enclosed. Of course, it would be a tremendous area to enclose. How big is the Game Reserve, Daddy?"

"The guide-book says that it covers an area of eight thousand square miles," said Daddy, "it's over two hundred miles long, and about forty miles wide."

"Why is it called the Kruger National Park?" asked Billy.

"Because it was President Kruger who first suggested that they should set aside a stretch of country as a Game reserve, when he saw how fast the wild animals were being killed off. But it wasn't until many years later that his suggestion was carried out."

As they drove along the gravel road between large plantations of beautiful trees, Penny's spirits soon began to rise and she started to sing,

> *All things bright and beautiful,*
> *All creatures great and small,*
> *All things wise and wonderful,*
> *The Lord God made them all.*

That was the hymn that the children had sung at the Sunday School which Dr. Mason had held in camp on the Sunday afternoon.

"At the Sunday School," said Penny, "Glenny's daddy

asked us which was the biggest animal we had seen in the Reserve. Some of the children said 'Elephant,' and some of them said 'Giraffe'."

"I think that those who said 'Elephant', were right," said Mummy.

"But some giraffes are taller than elephants," said Billy.

"Yes, but in bulk the elephants have it every time. I shall never forget that one we saw outside the Letaba Camp, it was simply *huge*," said Daddy.

"Yes," said Mummy, "and we were so close to it—much too close for my liking."

"But it didn't do anything to us," said Penny, "it just went on pulling leaves off the tree and eating them."

"Yes, mercifully it didn't pay any attention to us. I've certainly never seen such a big one before, it was like the side of a house."

"Did Mummy tell you that we had quite a fright with one elephant?" asked Glenny. "It was down near the Sabi river, before we had met you."

"Do tell us about it," said Penny, "what happened?"

"We were going along on that road that runs beside the river. We were going very slowly, because Daddy said that by a river was a likely place to see animals because they had to go there to drink. We had just turned a bend in the road, when suddenly there was a crashing noise in the bushes that were between us and the actual river. The next minute a big bull elephant stepped out of them on to the road right in front of our car."

"Oh, dear!" gasped Penny, "whatever did you do?"

"Well, it gave us a shock, and I think the elephant was just as surprised as we were. Daddy jammed on his brakes and we stopped right near the elephant."

"Oooooh!" cried Penny, "weren't you frightened?"

"I was a little bit," admitted Glenny honestly, "and so was Mummy, but Daddy wasn't. He snatched up his camera and began to take a picture of the elephant, but we were too close to get it all in. It got angry then and began to flap its ears at us, and it tossed its trunk up in the air and made a trumpeting noise at us. I was scared. Daddy said he would have backed the car away from it if he could, but he couldn't because, you see, we had just come round a bend in the road."

"So what did you do?" asked Billy.

"We didn't do anything, 'cos we couldn't. Mummy says that she really thought that the elephant was going to charge our car. But just at the last moment, it changed its mind and suddenly turned and dashed back into the bushes and down to the river-bed again."

"What a mercy!" said Mummy. "I'm glad we didn't have an experience like that."

"How many elephants did we see altogether, Billy?" asked Penny.

"I've got them all down in my book," said Billy, "I must count them up."

"Yes," said Daddy, "when we stop for lunch, we'll sort out Billy's lists and make a final survey of all the animals that we saw in the Reserve."

On they went, and soon the children gave up looking for any more wild animals.

"There's nothing now but sheep and cows and goats," said Billy in disgust.

"Let's pretend that they're wild animals," said Penny.

"Yes, let's," said Glenny, "look at that zebra," she said, pointing to a mangy-looking donkey.

Both girls giggled. "And look at that buffalo," said Penny, pointing to a cow.

Warming to their game, Glenny cried, "And here comes a jackal," and she pointed to a scraggy-looking dog who rushed out from a kraal to bark at them as they passed.

"It's a silly game," said Billy who wouldn't join in, "just like girls to play it," he added scornfully.

"It's not silly," said Penny, "it's fun."

"Now don't quarrel, children," said Mummy, and, changing the subject, she suggested,

"Let's each say which was our favourite animal that we saw in the Reserve. I'll start, and I say the graceful little mpala buck was mine."

"And that baby giraffe that we saw was my favourite," said Penny without any hesitation.

"The lion was my favourite of course," said Billy a little scornfully, "the big one with the mane."

"And you, Glenny?" asked Mrs. Dawson, "what was your favourite?"

"I'm thinking," said Glenny, "I can't make up my mind between two. We saw some little grey monkeys one day, bluey grey they were."

"I know," said Billy, "the vervet monkey."

"Don't interrupt," said Penny, "go on, Glenny."

"Well, there was a baby one with a little pink face, it was the sweetest little monkey I've ever seen. I don't know whether to choose that as my favourite, or the *beautiful* leopard that we saw; it had dark spots all over it's coat and lovely white whiskers."

"Well, make up your mind," said Billy, "you can't have them both."

After much whispering on the part of the two little

girls, Glenny decided in favour of the little vervet monkey.

"Now Daddy, it's your turn," said Penny.

"Well," said Daddy, "I'm in the same difficulty that Glenny was, I'm trying to decide between that magnificent kudu bull that we saw with those wor lerful spiral horns, and that cheetah that stood and posed for us in the middle of the road, you remember?"

"Oh yes," said Penny, "that was a lovely one."

"I think though, that I'll decide on the kudu bull," said Daddy finally.

Penny's usual cheerful spirits were quite restored by now and she started to sing, "I'm going exploring."

"You can't sing that any more," said Billy, "there's nothing more to explore, it's just the road now right up to Rhodesia."

"Oh, but all sorts of exciting things can happen on the rest of our journey," said Mummy, "I don't see why Penny can't still sing her 'exploring' song if she wants to."

"Yes, why not?" said Daddy, "we're all set now for Rhodesia."

"I know," said Penny suddenly, "now I can sing, 'I'm going to Rhodesia' instead," and she started right off to sing her new words.

"The same old tune," groaned Billy, who was still feeling a bit disgruntled.

"You're just jealous," said Penny "'cos you can't sing yourself."

It was a sad fact that Billy couldn't sing a note, at least, not in tune; he simply had no ear for music at all. But it was too bad of Penny to tease him about it, for it was always a sore point.

"I don't see why Penny has to keep on singing all the time," grumbled Billy, "first 'I'm going a-sailing,' then 'I'm going exploring'—and now 'I'm going to Rhodesia.' There's no end to it."

"Penny sings because she's happy, and we like to hear her," said Mummy. "What do you do when you're happy and want to express it?"

"I yell, of course," said Billy, "or shout."

"It's better to sing than to yell, isn't it Glenny?" said Penny.

"Oh, yes," said Glenny who was very loyal to her friend and would have supported her either way.

"Still," said Mummy, "you must each express your happiness in your own way, and let the other do so too. And now no more disagreements please; we are nearly at the lunch-place and I hope you are all hungry."

"I'm starving," said Penny and Glenny and Billy, all with one voice.

CHAPTER II

SILVER QUEEN TO THE RESCUE

LIFE wasn't quite as flat as Billy feared although they had left the exciting Game Reserve behind, for that very afternoon they had an adventure which even cheered up Billy.

They all enjoyed their picnic-lunch by the roadside very much. They had stopped at a place where there were some fine shady trees, and near a bridge under which a cheerful little stream gurgled along. The children were enchanted to have the opportunity to play for a little while beside this stream. But they could not stay long as they still had a long way to go to the place where they were to spend the night.

"And, what is more," added Daddy, "we have to climb and climb and climb this afternoon and go over a high mountain pass in the Magoebaskloof range. I hear that the scenery is very beautiful all the way from here to the border."

So, having filled up the radiator with water from the little stream, they went on their way again. Sure enough, almost at once, the road started to climb and to wind round and round the mountain-side.

"I don't like looking over the edge where it is such a steep drop down on this side," said Mummy.

"Well, don't look then," said Daddy, "look at the mountain-side."

It was all very beautiful, whichever way they looked.

"We must stop when we get to the top," cried Mummy, "and enjoy the view."

"We'll have to stop anyway," said Daddy, "to let our engine cool down a bit. I must say the Silver Queen is a splendid climber."

"Our car is a good climber too," said Glenny, looking back through the rear window and seeing her daddy's car keeping up well behind them.

Long before they got to the top, however, they turned a bend in the road and saw a bay going off the road on the inside. Here a small car had come to a standstill and beside it stood two young ladies with anxious looks on their faces.

When he saw them, Mr. Dawson pulled his car off the road and drew up in front of the small car, and Dr. Mason followed and drew his car up behind the little car and stopped.

They got out and went over to the young ladies.

"Are you in trouble?" they asked, "and if so, can we help?"

Relief showed on the faces of the young ladies as the taller and older one replied,

"Oh, thank you so much; yes, we're stuck. Our engine started giving a bit of trouble a little way back, and we saw that the water in the radiator was boiling, so we drew in to this side bay and stopped it to give it a chance to cool down. Then when we wanted to go on again, it simply wouldn't start. We've tried and tried, but can't get it going again."

"Don't worry," said Mr. Dawson, "we'll see if we can help."

They opened up the bonnet of the little car and soon both men were engrossed in checking up the engine. Here Billy joined them and tried to look as knowledgeable as his elders.

"Of course," said the taller young lady, "our car is rather old."

"Yes," put in Billy, "it's a—"

"Now no rude remarks," said his father, and the uncomplimentary observation that Billy was about to make was nipped in the bud.

The young lady smiled at Billy and said,

"I see you've got a lovely new car."

"Yes," he said eagerly, "it's a Vauxhall, the latest model. We've come all the way from Cape Town in her."

"And we came all the way from Cape Town in our little car," said the young lady.

Billy looked at the little old car with a new respect when he heard that.

"And, what is more," she continued, "we hope to go all the way back to Cape Town in her for that is where we live."

Just then Mrs. Dawson and Mrs. Mason and the two little girls came over and joined them.

"By the way," said the taller young lady, laughing, "we haven't introduced ourselves to you yet. This is my sister Jennifer Jordan, and my name is Margaret Jordan. How do you do?"

The ladies acknowledged their greeting and proceeded to introduce themselves and their husbands to the two girls.

"And this is Penny and her friend Glenny."

"And I'm Billy," said that young man, determined not to be left out, then, turning suddenly shy, he disappeared under the bonnet of the car.

"It's very kind of you all to stop and help us," said Margaret Jordan, "we were just getting desperate because so many cars passed us without stopping."

"I suggest," said Mr. Dawson, "that you ladies go and sit in the shade over there. Aren't there some cold drinks in our car, Mummy, what about having one while you are waiting?"

"Yes," said Margaret, "and there are some sweets in 'Dorcas' that the children might like, get them out, Jenny."

"What is 'Dorcas'?" asked Penny.

"That's the name of our little car. We named her after a lady in the Bible who, it is said, was 'full of good works'! Our car was certainly full of good works, too, but she is getting a bit on the aged side now I'm afraid."

"Our car's name is 'Silver Queen'," said Penny.

"A very nice name too," laughed Jennifer, "and that's just what she looks like."

The ladies settled themselves down under the shade of some trees and were soon chatting away as though they were all old friends.

"We've had a lovely time in the Game Reserve," said Margaret, "I suppose that's where you've come from too."

"Yes," said Penny, "we were so sad when we left it this morning. Did you see any lions? We did."

"Lions!" exclaimed Margaret, "I should think we did! We had a great thrill with lions."

"Do tell us about it," said Mummy.

"Well," said Jennifer, "we were staying in the Satara camp and one day my sister decided to stay in camp and cook our lunch but she urged me to take a little run round looking for animals while she did so."

"So off I went on one of the roads there. At first I didn't see anything at all and there weren't even any other cars on the road. I began to think that I had made a mistake going on that road, and that I ought to turn back. Just then I turned a corner and in the distance I saw what I thought was a barrier put across the road. So I thought, 'Well, I shall have to turn when I get up to that and go back.' But when I got close to it, what *do* you think I found?"

Penny and Glenny both breathed, "What?"

"Right across the road was a dead wildebeest and round it I counted ten lions! A big old male lion with a thick mane was lying in the road in front, he had evidently had his fill and was now on guard while the lioness and the big cubs had their lunch. The latter were tucking in for all they were worth and took no notice of me, but the old lion watched me carefully to see what I was going to do."

"And what did you do?" asked Penny.

"To tell you the truth, I was quite frightened. It was the first time I had seen lions so close, and ten of them! Then I realised what a thrill my sister was missing, so I turned the car round and went back to the camp as quickly as I could to fetch her. On the way I stopped and told the people in every car I met, and also I told the people in the camp. The result was that people flocked out to see the great sight. By the time we got back, there was very little left of the wildebeest, and the lioness and cubs were sitting or lying about, licking their chops after their nice meal."

"Poor wildebeest!" said Penny whose sympathies always went out to those who got the worst of it.

Just then the men-folk came over to confess that they had not been able to get the little car started.

"But I have a steel tow-rope with me," said Mr. Dawson, "I suggest that we tow you up the rest of the mountain and on to the pass, then perhaps we can get her started on the downward grade."

"Oh, thank you so much," said Margaret, "it is kind of you to go to all this trouble for us."

"Not at all!" said Mr. Dawson, "it would be a pity if we couldn't help a stranded fellow-traveller."

While the tow-rope was being adjusted between the two cars, Penny and Glenny between them were telling Billy about the wonderful adventure that the young ladies had had with the lions. Billy was envious when he heard it.

"My! I wished that had happened to us!" he said.

The two Miss Jordans got into their car, Miss Margaret steering and the Dawson's car set off pulling them up behind her nicely. Mummy and Penny and Glenny all got into the Mason's car and followed on behind. In due course they all arrived at the top of the mountain pass and, pulling their cars off the main part of the road they stopped.

Mummy went into raptures over the wonderful views as soon as she stepped out of the car, and so did the other ladies. It certainly was magnificent to see range after range of mountains rolling away into the distance, with charming little fertile green valleys in between them.

"Look at the road we have come on," said Dr. Mason, and there it stretched for miles behind them, looking like a thin white ribbon winding and twisting into the distance.

But Dr. Mason and Mr. Dawson were not interested in the view for long, they were having another shot at starting the little car.

"I've just had an idea," said Dr. Mason. "Have you got a cloth and some cold water? We might try putting a compress on the petrol pipe here as it may be an air-lock."

B

"I've got a cloth," said Margaret, "but no water."

"There's some lemonade left in one of the bottles," said Mummy, "would that do?"

"Yes," said Dr. Mason, "why not, it's wet and cold."

"What a waste of a cold drink!" Billy was heard to mutter.

"Not if it gets our car started," said Jennifer.

Anyway, whether it was due to the lemonade compress or what, no-one knows, but certain it was that in a little while, the engine of the small car gave a splutter and then started.

"Hurrah!" shouted Billy, and everyone was pleased.

The two girls were profuse in their thanks as they said their 'Goodbyes' all round. They were anxious to get going before the engine stopped again. They handed a card to Mrs. Dawson and said, "If you ever come to Cape Town again, be sure and look us up; we should be so pleased to see you."

"And we must thank the Silver Queen too," said Jennifer, "for so kindly pulling us up that steep road," and she patted the bonnet of the grey car as she spoke, "she has behaved like a real queen to us to-day."

Away they went in fine style down the hill and towards the road which would take them to Johannesburg on their way back to Cape Town.

"Goodbye, Goodbye," waved Penny and Glenny, until the little car was right out of sight.

"Well, that's a good thing done," said Mr. Dawson, wiping his hands on a rag and tidying up generally, "I'm glad we were able to help them."

"It was our Silver Queen who helped them, wasn't it?" said Penny.

"It certainly was," said Daddy, "and now we must get

going or the sun will set before we reach our sleeping-place." They jumped into their cars and were soon speeding away to the north, in the opposite direction from that taken by the little car.

CHAPTER III

CROSSING THE BORDER

THE sun was just preparing to set in a rosy glow away on the western horizon when the travellers arrived at the Motel where they had arranged to spend the night. It was called the Lalapanzi Motel and it was on the Great North road.

"What's the difference between a hotel and a motel?" asked Glenny.

"I don't really know, dear," said Mrs. Dawson, "except that the motels seem to have their bedrooms in the form of separate rondhavels, and you pay for your sleeping accommodation separately from your meals. But this looks a lovely place."

The ground in between the rondhavels had been cultivated into pretty little gardens, and at that time of the year, the whole place was gay with brightly coloured flowers, canna lilies, and zinnias and marigolds, and the homely nasturtiums. Aubretia flourished in the rockeries, and verbena bordered the flagged paths which connected the rondhavels with each other and with the dining-saloon and other buildings.

"Lalapanzi's a funny name," said Penny.

"Yes," said Mummy, "I asked about it when we came in and they say that it's a native word and it means 'Sleep here'."

"And that's just what we're going to do, aren't we?" said Penny.

"Yes," said Mummy, who was busy unpacking the things that they needed for the night, "that's, as you say, just what we're going to do, and the sooner you are in your beds, my children, the better, for you have had a long and exciting day."

Even as she spoke, the supper gong sounded; it was a musical one which a little African boy dressed in a smart red suit was sounding as he walked round the paths between the huts.

The children hurried to wash their hands and faces and brush their hair, and then they all went over to supper.

It was a lovely supper and the travellers did full justice to the good things provided. There was soup and fish and roast duckling with green peas, followed by fruit jelly and custard.

By the time they had finished their meal it was quite dark, but when they emerged from the dining-saloon, the children were delighted to find that the paths to the huts were lit by prettily coloured lanterns hung between the trees.

"Oh, look Mummy," said Penny, "it's like the party we had on the boat coming out from England, the coloured lights that we had on the deck."

Billy went off to play ping-pong for a while with some of the other boys staying at the Motel, but the two little girls were quite ready for bed. The rondhavels that they had were next door to each other. They were very gay huts, the woodwork of each being painted in bright colours, all different. Penny was pleased because the hut that her family had was painted in blue which was her favourite colour. The hut that the Masons had was painted in green.

"Goodnight, Glenny," said Penny to her friend when they came to the parting of the ways.

"Goodnight, Penny," Glenny replied, "sleep tight, and don't dream about the poor wildebeest that the lions ate, will you?"

"I hope not," said Penny. She fell asleep as soon as her head touched the pillow and she didn't dream about anything at all.

The next morning they were wakened by the little African boy in the red suit bringing in their early morning coffee. The children jumped up at once and got dressed and went out to play in the garden until breakfast time.

After breakfast they soon got the suitcases packed into the cars, for they were eager to be off and on their way once more.

"This is a very important day in our journey," said Mr. Dawson, "because to-day we leave the country of South Africa and enter into our new country of Rhodesia. Isn't that exciting?"

"I'm going to Rhodesia," sang Penny happily as she skipped along the path.

"So am I," said Glenny, "you're going to Southern Rhodesia, and Mummy and Daddy and I are going to Northern Rhodesia."

The two little girls were suddenly sobered by the thought that to-day they would have to say 'Goodbye' to each other, for, once they crossed the Border, the Masons would have to take the road which goes to Bulawayo and on north, while the Dawson family would take the road which goes to Salisbury where their new home was to be.

They set off after breakfast on the Great North road again and, after climbing for a while, the road started to drop down, down, down, winding through a deep gap in the mountains.

"This narrow gap is called a 'poort' in South Africa," Daddy explained to the children, "it's a sort of gorge." The scenery was beautiful and, at one place, they stopped the car by a little bridge right down at the bottom of the dip. The children ran down to the small stream that went through the valley there, while their elders sat on the bridge wall and munched some Golden Delicious apples.

"Well," said Mr. Dawson, "we shall soon have to part company with you now, we, to go to our new life in Salisbury, and you to go back to your home and work in the mission-field."

"Yes," said Dr. Mason, "we are longing now to get back to our Lamba people, among whom we work. We have had a wonderful holiday and feel fine after it and ready for the fray once more."

"It must be a lonely life for you in some ways," said Mrs. Dawson, "how many white people are there on your station?"

"There are just five of us, not counting Glenny," said Dr. Mason, "our two selves, two nurses and a teacher. But we are always so busy that we don't have much time to feel lonely."

"How long will it take you to reach your mission-station?" Mr. Dawson asked Dr. Mason.

"Four or five days, if we are not held up anywhere en route," the doctor replied. "And you? When do you expect to get to Salisbury?"

"In about three days' time, because we are planning to spend one day looking at the Zimbabwe Ruins."

"You'll find those very interesting," said Dr. Mason, "we visited them once."

"And now it is time that we were moving," said Mr. Dawson. "The Customs place at Beit Bridge will be open and the sooner we get there the better. Come children," he called to Penny and Billy and Glenny.

They came running up from the river.

"We saw a lizard with a blue head," announced Penny, "but it ran behind some rocks and we couldn't find it again."

"There are lots of those lizards up in Rhodesia," said Glenny.

"Yes," said her Daddy, "and you'll see the little grey lizard too. When it is chased by an enemy it calmly sheds its tail and runs off without it; I've often seen them running around without tails, but they grow new ones again in time."

They got into the cars and proceeded on their way to Beit Bridge. After they emerged from the Poort, the country was flat and uninteresting. But now they noticed a lot of funny shaped trees which they had not seen before. They had very fat grey trunks from which the branches shot out in weird shapes and directions.

"Whatever are those funny trees?" asked Penny.

"They must be the baobabs," said her Daddy, "they *are* strange looking, aren't they? Of course, being winter, they have no leaves on just now, I don't suppose they look so strange when they are covered in foliage in the summer."

"Their trunks are huge," said Mummy, "and I see that it says in this guide-book that some African tribes used to have the custom of burying their dead inside the hollow trunks of these tress. How horrible!"

"Some people call them 'cream of tartar' trees,' said Daddy, "I don't know why."

"That's the stuff that Mummy puts in the scones, isn't it, Mummy?" asked Penny.

"Yes, but it doesn't come from these trees, surely," said Mummy.

They did not stop again until they reached the little town of Messina which was very near the border. Here they drew up at a garage for petrol.

"This is a mining town," said Dr. Mason, "copper and other minerals. It's a terribly hot place."

"Then I'm glad we are not going to live here," said Mummy.

They did not linger, but hurried on and in a few minutes they came in sight of the very fine Beit Bridge which spans the Limpopo river. The latter is the boundary between South Africa and Rhodesia. It was Billy who spotted the bridge first.

"There's the bridge," he shouted, "I saw it first."

They drew up in the parking places provided for cars outside the Customs and Immigration building. The two men went inside with the passports and other papers, while the ladies sat in the car and talked, and the children ran about to see all that there was to be seen.

It seemed a very long time till Mr. Dawson and Dr. Mason came out again.

"I'm sorry we've been so long," said Mr. Dawson. "So many questions were asked about the car and there were forms to fill in."

Once back in the cars, an African policeman lifted a big wooden boom across the road and let them through. They drove slowly across the bridge, and halfway over they halted for a minute to look at a big granite memorial to Mr. Alfred Beit who was so generous in financing this and other schemes for the benefit and advancement of Rhodesia.

When they reached the other side, Daddy said triumphantly, "Now we are in Rhodesia."

"I'm in Rhodesia," sang Penny happily as the cars made their way up to the hotel which was only a short distance from the Bridge.

"What about a cup of coffee together before we have to part?" suggested Mr. Dawson.

"That's a grand idea," the others agreed.

They sat down at a table covered by a gay little cloth, in the garden in front of the Beit Bridge Hotel. Around them were brightly-coloured flowers of all sorts. Mummy was greatly taken with a beautiful creeper over an archway which had a profusion of orange coloured blossoms.

"That is called 'Golden Shower'," said Dr. Mason, "it's really a big sort of honey-suckle; it grows everywhere in the tropics and makes a lovely show at this time of the year."

Glenny and Penny were feeling very subdued now, they didn't like the thought of parting from each other at all. After they had finished their cold drinks, they walked about with their arms round each others necks, promising never to forget each other.

Then came the inevitable parting. The Dawsons accompanied the Masons to the cross-roads where a signpost pointing to the left said, 'To Bulawayo', and a signpost pointing to the right said, 'To Salisbury'.

"So we've come to the parting of the ways," said Dr. Mason, "we shall miss you for the rest of our journey."

"And we shall miss you too," said Mummy, "it has been lovely travelling together since we met again in the Reserve."

"I don't know what I shall do without Glenny," said Penny dismally.

"Never mind," said Daddy, "we may meet again some day, who knows?"

'Goodbyes' were said all round, then the Masons started up their car and away they went with Glenny leaning out of the window and waving her hankie until a bend in the road swept them out of sight.

"And that," said Daddy, "is that. And now off we go."

They got into the Silver Queen, and, taking the other road, set off for Fort Victoria and Salisbury.

CHAPTER IV

THE ZIMBABWE RUINS

"OH, what a funny road!" exclaimed Penny soon after they started.

And indeed, it did look strange, for this was the first time they had travelled on 'strips'. The road was an ordinary gravel one with just two strips of tarmac for the car wheels.

"It *is* a funny road, as you say, Penny," said her Daddy after a few minutes, "and it's not going to be so easy to drive on. To keep on these strips I'll have to concentrate on the road all the time, and we can't go so quickly as we have been doing."

"What happens when a car comes from the other direction and wants to pass us?" asked Billy.

"Then I must give them one of the strips and go over to this side," said Daddy.

The children were interested in this idea and waited anxiously for a car to come and pass them. It was quite a while before one appeared, they seemed to have the whole world to themselves for a long time. Then Penny's sharp eyes spotted a car in the distance.

The children watched eagerly as it came nearer, then, sure enough it turned off to its side having one wheel now in the dust at the side of the road, and the other on a tarmac strip. Daddy did the same on their side, and in a moment the two cars flashed past each other raising a cloud of dust as they did so.

"That's fun," said Billy, "I hope another car comes soon."

"It may be fun for you," said Daddy, "but not so much for the driver. If we keep on having to do that I don't know when we shall reach our destination."

"What's destination, Daddy?" asked Penny, stumbling over the long word.

"The place we're making for," said Daddy, "where we are going to sleep to-night."

"And where is that?" asked Billy.

"The Shepherd's Hotel, by the Zimbabwe Ruins," said Daddy.

After mid-day they crossed a big river which had some nice shady trees on the other side of the bridge.

"I think this would be a good place to stop and have our lunch," said Mummy.

"Yes, I'm hungry," said Billy.

"Oh, you're always hungry," cried Penny. "I'm not."

But all the same, when Mummy had spread a plastic cloth on the grass and produced the egg sandwiches and sausage rolls which they had brought from the Motel, Penny found that she was quite able to eat her full share of them. Afterwards they had lovely ripe golden bananas grown in Natal, and while Mummy and Daddy enjoyed tea from a thermos flask, Penny and Billy had a bottle of coco-cola each.

Then they were on their way again for there was no time to linger. By the time that they reached the place where the road turns off to the Ruins, it was quite late in the afternoon.

"It's not far now to the hotel," said Daddy, "and I'm glad we are on a decent gravel road again without strips, I don't like those stripped roads at all."

The sun was setting as they drew up in front of the Shepherd's hotel, and seen through some large old clusters of sisal bushes, it was a lovely sight. Even Penny who had fallen asleep, woke up now to admire the view. Then they hurried into the hotel and soon they were in their comfortable rooms and getting ready for supper.

"I wonder where Glenny is now," said Penny when her mother was tucking her up for the night.

"In Bulawayo, I expect," said Mummy.

"I wish she was going to live in Salisbury," said Penny, "I won't know any girls there."

"Oh, but you will soon make friends with other little girls there," said Mummy. "It's much worse for Glenny, she has no other little white girls where she lives. I expect she plays with some of the little African girls."

In her prayers that night, Penny asked God to bless Glenny and the little African girls that she played with.

The next day, the Dawson family set off to explore the great Zimbabwe Ruins. How surprised they were when they saw how big they were! Great blocks of stone were piled one on top of the other forming tremendous walls, and there was no mortar or cement between the layers of stones.

"Why! This is wonderful," cried Daddy. "Whoever can have put up these gigantic walls? And to think they have stood for hundreds, perhaps thousands of years!"

"Why, Dad, who *did* build them?" asked Billy.

"Ah, that's the mystery," replied Daddy, "no-one knows who built them, or when, or for what purpose. It's a puzzle that has never yet been solved."

"How exciting!" said Billy, gazing with awe at the vast ruins.

"Some authorities," Daddy went on, "think that they date back for three thousand years to the time when King Solomon lived on earth."

"The one in the Bible?" asked Billy.

"Yes," said Daddy, "it says that Solomon sent to Ophir for gold, and some think that this is that place. They have actually found evidence here of a crude sort of gold-mining."

"How wonderful if it is so!" said Mummy. "I was only reading in the Bible the other day how King Solomon made a navy of ships and sent them to fetch gold and apes and peacocks and spices and ivory."

"I expect the 'apes' were gorillas," said Billy.

"I'd like to have seen the peacocks," said Penny. "There were lovely ones at the Zoo, specially when they spread their tails out."

"But," said Daddy, consulting the guide-book, "others say that the Ruins are of much later date, and that it was Africans who built them, but no-one really knows."

Just then a guide came along, and several other people had gathered near by.

"Good morning, sir," said the guide, "would you like to join a party going round the Ruins?"

"Yes, please, we would," said Daddy, "they are most interesting, though no-one seems to know much about them."

"That's right, sir," said the guide, "it's all shrouded in the mystery of the past."

"Then who gave them the name of Zimbabwe?" asked Daddy.

"Oh, that is just the local African word for stones or ruins," said the guide, "it doesn't help us at all."

When the people had all come together, the guide said, "We will go up to the Acropolis first before it gets too hot, it's quite a pull up to the top of that hill."

The people trooped after the guide, picking their way

carefully on the rough stony ground and up the rather steep path.

"Oh, what a wonderful view!" exclaimed Mummy when they got to the top, "you can see for miles around."

"Yes," said the guide, "the Acropolis was probably designed for defence, that's why it's on this granite hill with a good view of all the approaches to the place."

"Penny," called Billy in a stage whisper.

When Penny turned back to him, Billy said, "We don't want to listen to all this stuff, let's go off and play in that part down there where those other children are." Nothing loth, Penny went with Billy, and they slipped away down the path to another part of the Ruins. This was full of narrow passages winding in and out of the great walls, and had fascinating little towers on the top of the wall at one side.

It was an ideal place to play hide and seek and other games, and soon Penny and Billy had joined some other children whose parents were in the guide's party, and they had great fun chasing each other through the narrow passages, and hiding in the tunnels.

"My daddy says this used to be a fort in the old days," said one little boy. Billy looked up at the towers, and in his imagination he could see the soldiers of long ago manning these battlements and defending it against the enemy coming up from the valley below.

"I know what," he said eagerly to the others, "let's pretend we're soldiers, some of you go outside, and the rest of us will keep you from getting in."

The boys in the party entered eagerly into this new game, but Penny found it a bit rough and wandered back to look for Mummy.

CHAPTER V

TO FORT VICTORIA

PENNY met the party coming down from the Acropolis, and joined her Mummy who was talking to another lady. This lady had with her a dear little girl about three years old. She had golden curls all over her head and the bluest of blue eyes, and when she smiled up at Penny, two lovely dimples appeared in her cheeks.

"Oh, you darling!" said Penny, taking one of her little hands.

"This is my little daughter Penny," said Mummy to the other lady whose name was Mrs. Dennis.

"And this is Linda," said Mrs. Dennis, introducing her little girl.

"Oh," said Penny, "I've got a dolly named Belinda, but I call her Linda for short."

"Well," said Mrs. Dennis, "here is a real live dolly for you to play with if you like."

They had been walking towards a little café where the party were going to have morning tea. The Dawsons and Mrs. Dennis sat down at one table, and Penny and Linda sat on the grass and played.

"Where's Billy?" asked Daddy.

"He's playing soldiers with the other boys over there," said Penny. "It's a lovely place to play in."

"We'll leave him then, but if he doesn't come soon he won't get any ice-cream."

Lovely ice-creams of different sorts were served as well as tea and coffee. Needless to say, Penny chose a pink ice-cream with slices of banana in it, but she fed quite half of it to little Linda who smacked her lips over it and enjoyed it very much.

Just as the people were ready to move on again with the guide to another part of the Ruins, Billy and the other boys came running up hot and red in the face after the battles they had had.

"*We've* had lovely ice-cream," announced Penny, "pink ones with banana in."

"Aw!" said Billy looking disappointed.

"It's too late now to get those, but go and get yourselves some ice-cream cones," said Mummy, giving Billy some money. Off ran the boys, and the rest of the people went off with the guide to visit the part of the Ruins that is called 'The Temple'.

But Mrs. Dennis decided to go back to the hotel with little Linda and Penny elected to go with them.

After lunch it was so very hot that everyone felt that they wanted to have a snooze until tea-time, except the children who were allowed to play in the hotel garden as long as they did not make too much noise, and kept in the shady parts.

Later on, to her great joy, Penny was invited by Mrs. Dennis to go and see Linda have her bath, and it wasn't until the little one was safely tucked up in her cot for the night, that Penny could be persuaded to leave her.

"Only one more day's journey," said Daddy at supper-time that evening, "and then our travels will be over. We should reach Salisbury to-morrow afternoon, won't that be exciting?"

"It seems simply ages since we left England," said Mummy, "I suppose that is because so much has happened since then and we have seen so many places and met so many people."

"If we hadn't come here," said Penny, "I shouldn't have met dear little Linda."

"I must say I shall be glad when we have finished with packing and unpacking our suit-cases," said Mummy. "After a time one gets tired of living in boxes, it will be quite nice to get settled in a house again."

"Have we got a house in Salisbury?" asked Billy.

"Not yet," said Daddy, "we will go into a hotel when we arrive there, until we know what the firm has been able to arrange for us."

"I'm glad we are going to live in Rhodesia," said Billy, "it's summer all the year round here, I know, because one of those boys at the Ruins told me. He lives in Salisbury."

"I expect we shall be homesick for dear old England sometimes," said Mummy wistfully. "Still I'm sure we shall all be very happy in our new country once we get settled down."

"And what about you, my Poppet?" said Daddy to Penny.

"I don't mind, Daddy," said Penny, "as long as I'm with you and Mummy and Billy, I don't mind where it is."

"That's my sensible little girl," said Daddy, "and now it's bedtime for little people."

"Oh, please, can't we play for a little while in the Games room," begged Penny, "there's all sorts of lovely things in there?"

"All right," said Daddy, "but as soon as Mummy calls, you must come. Meantime, we can get our packing done in peace."

Off the children ran to the Games Room and were soon involved in a game of Progressive Ping-pong with some of the other children.

The next morning they had a last glimpse of the Zimbabwe Ruins standing up starkly in the grey morning light when, after a very early breakfast, they passed them on their way to Fort Victoria.

When they reached this little town, they had to take the Silver Queen to a garage to be investigated for a mysterious noise which she had developed.

"Never mind," said Daddy, "it will give us a chance to look at this interesting little place which, according to my book, is the oldest established town in S. Rhodesia. Apparently it was originally just a fort, named after Queen Victoria by the Pioneer Column who built it."

"What's the Pioneer Column?" asked Penny.

"I'm not very sure, darling," said Daddy, "you see, it's all as new to me as it is to you and I only know what is in this guide-book here."

"Excuse me," said a voice behind them, and they turned to see an old man, sitting on a wall. To the eyes of Penny and Billy he seemed to be a very, very old man for he had a long white beard, and faded blue eyes which had not, however, lost their twinkle.

"Why," thought Penny to herself, "he looks just like Father Christmas," but, of course, she did not say this out loud.

"Excuse me," said the old man again in a quavering voice, "but I couldn't help hearing the little girl's question. May I tell you about the Pioneer Column?"

"Thank you," said Daddy, "that would be very kind of you. Our car is in the garage needing a little attention, and we thought we would like to look round this place; we are strangers here on our way to Salisbury."

"We've come all the way from England," piped up Penny.

"Have you indeed, little Missy? well, so did I once upon a time, but it was a long, long time ago. I came from Cornwall."

"But this is a most interesting little place, and as you have got to spend a little time here waiting for your car, I'll tell you a little bit about it."

"Is it a story?" asked Penny looking up hopefully into the face of the old man.

"A story!" exclaimed their new friend, "I should just think it *is* a story! What about you coming and sitting on this wall by me, little lady, and you the other side, my boy, and then you can hear all about it."

Penny was hoisted to a seat on the wall on one side of the old man while Billy lolled against the wall on the other side, both of them eager to hear the story which the old man had to tell them.

CHAPTER VI

THE STORY

"ONCE upon a time," the old man began, "there was a man named Cecil John Rhodes."

"I know," burst in Penny, "we saw him in the Gardens in Cape Town."

"Well," said the old man with a twinkle in his eye, "he has been dead for quite a while now—"

"It was his monument we saw," explained Billy, "and he was pointing up to the north."

"Quite right, young man, he was pointing up here to where we are now. You see, Rhodes wasn't satisfied with getting South Africa for his queen and country, he looked up to this part of Africa which at that time was all wild unexplored country, and he wanted this too for Britain. He was a man of vision."

What's vision?" asked Penny.

"Oh, dear, Penny," said Mummy, "must you ask so many questions?"

"Of course she must, my dear madam," said the old man, "how else can the children learn if they don't ask questions? You should have heard my small grandson with his questions—no end to them! And when he had me stumped and I finally said to one question, 'I don't know', he said, '*Why* don't you know, Grandpa'?

"But, to get back to our story, Rhodes was a man who looked ahead and saw things in the future that he wanted to happen, and one of these things was that this country should be opened up. So he made an agreement with the big Chief who ruled over the Matabele natives. This Chief's name was Lobengula. Rhodes made an agreement with him that white men should be allowed to come into his country and look for things like gold and copper and other minerals.

"Then Rhodes picked out a band of about two hundred special young men to come up to this country to spy out the land and see what it was like, and open it up."

"Like the spies in the Bible," said Penny.

"That's right," said the old man, "only there were two hundred of them instead of twelve.

"These young men were very brave. They endured great hardships travelling through this unknown country. They had to hack their way through dense forests, they had to swim across rivers that were full of crocodiles; they were in danger from lions and leopards and elephants and other wild animals, not to mention snakes. They got sick with fever and other strange diseases, and above all they went in terror of the Matabele natives who attacked them whenever they could.

"These young men were called the Pioneer Column that I heard you asking about just now. They marched on and on; in spite of all the dangers and hardships, the hunger and the thirst they endured, they would not turn back. They came right on till they climbed the mountains just below here. Then they got into a deep gorge and couldn't find their way out of it. Now they really were frightened, and they expected that any minute the natives would spring out and attack them and they would all be killed in that trap. But in the end they suddenly found a way through and into this lovely valley. They were so glad that they decided to stay right here for a while and they set to work and built a fort which they called Fort Victoria, after Queen Victoria.

"Of course the old fort has gone, all except the bell-tower which you will see down the street there. And still every day that bell in the tower is rung morning and evening and reminds the folk here of those brave pioneers who opened up this country.

"Then other white people came and after a while the natives of the country started attacking these new white people even though their Chief had agreed that the white people could come. There were lots of fights between them.

"One day a Major Allan Wilson and his patrol of eighteen soldiers were sent out after the Chief Lobengula. They came to a river called the Shangani River where they could see some of the wagons of the chief. Major Wilson and his men halted there at the river and called across to the chief, urging them to surrender.

"Suddenly from out of the forest around, dozens of natives sprang at Major Wilson and his men. The latter were so few and the natives were so many, but the white men didn't run away. Even though they knew that they were hopelessly outnumbered and hadn't a hope, every one of those nineteen Englishmen stood their ground and fought bravely against the attacking hordes of natives. They fought desperately until all their ammunition was finished and the natives closed in on that brave little patrol and killed them one by one.

"The last few of them could do nothing to defend themselves, and finally they sank on to their knees, and, raising their flag, they sang, or tried to sing, the British National Anthem, until they too were killed. Not one man was left of that brave little band of men."

The old man paused, and Penny heaved a great sigh, but Billy's eyes were shining as he thought of those brave men, these pioneers of this country of Rhodesia.

"And to-day," said Grandpa, "in this town of Fort Victoria, we have seventeen of our streets which are named after some of those pioneers. And up on the Matopo Hills, near Bulawayo, their bones are buried right near to the grave of Cecil Rhodes himself, and a fine memorial has been erected to Major Allan Wilson and his men. Perhaps you will see it one day, if you travel through Bulawayo."

"Isn't that a fine story?" asked the old man.

"Yes, indeed," said Mummy, "it is. Thank you so much for telling it to us, I'm sure the children will always remember it."

"That's the story of Fort Victoria," the old man said, "and we are all very proud of our Pioneer Column."

Just then Daddy, who had slipped away to go and see how things were getting on at the garage, came along and said, "Come along now, the Silver Queen is all ready, and we must be getting on our way."

Seeing the puzzled look on the old man's face, Penny explained "The Silver Queen is our car 'cos she's silver coloured and—and—"

"And behaves like a queen," finished Daddy.

"Oh, I see," and the old man smiled, and waved to them as they hurried off to the garage, leaving him to his seat in the sun and his memories of olden days.

CHAPTER VII

THE ACCIDENT

AFTER the Dawson family left Fort Victoria, the road continued northward, and they went steadily on until lunch-time. In Fort Victoria Mummy had bought some sausages, also some fresh rolls, and she had said to the children,

"What about having a sort of 'braavleis' when we stop for lunch?"

"Oh, yes," said Penny, "like we had in Johannesburg, that would be fun."

So, when Daddy had chosen a suitable place, Penny and Billy collected twigs and wood lying about in the forest and soon Billy had got a fire going in his best 'boy scout' style. Then out came the forks and they had great fun roasting their sausages over the fire, then clapping them between the rolls and eating them.

For sweets they had a lovely ripe sweet paw-paw which Mummy had also bought in Fort Victoria. They cut it into four parts, removed the seeds, sprinkled it with a little lemon juice, and eaten with a spoon it was just delicious.

"Now," said Daddy, "we must pack up quickly and get going again as we still have quite a long way to go."

"You can run down and wash the forks and cups in the river, children," said Mummy.

Penny and Billy thought that was good fun, washing up in the river. Unfortunately Penny dropped one of the cups into the part where the current was and it started sailing down the river quite fast. But Billy ran along the bank and managed to rescue it, so all was well.

As they got back into the car once more, Daddy said, "Now for the last lap of our long, long journey. By sunset we should be in Salisbury." But he little knew that still another adventure was to befall them before they arrived.

The road still had the strips stretching along it like yards of grey ribbon spread out on either side. As they were going along that afternoon at a steady pace, Billy said, "Daddy, there's a car right behind us, and I think they want to get past us, the man keeps hooting."

So Daddy moved over to his side, leaving one of the strips free for the car to overtake him, which they did right away, sending up showers of dust as they passed.

"Whew!" said Daddy, "that car is travelling much too fast for this sort of road, that driver could easily turn his car over if the wheels slipped off the strips while he is going at that speed."

"There was a little girl in that car," said Penny, "I saw her sitting in the back with a black lady."

"I expect that would be her Nanny," said Mummy.

The car that had passed them vanished quickly into the distance in a cloud of dust, and the Dawsons thought that they had seen the last of it, but they hadn't!

Later that afternoon, just when they were all getting excited at the thought of arriving shortly in Salisbury, they turned a bend in the road and there a little way in front of them they saw a car upside down in the road.

Daddy jammed his brakes on and brought their car to a standstill.

"It's only just happened," said Billy, "see, the wheels are still spinning round."

"It's the car that passed us," said Penny, horrified at seeing it turned over.

Daddy and Mummy jumped out of the car to go to help the people in the overturned car, and Billy was going too, but Mummy said, "No, Billy, you stay here with Penny, I don't want her to see anything gruesome. And Billy, get our First Aid box out, we may need it."

Billy wasn't at all pleased at having to stay behind, but he busied himself getting out the First Aid box.

"Oh, dear," said Penny anxiously, "I do hope that the little girl isn't hurt."

A minute or two later they saw Mummy coming back to them carrying the little girl in her arms. The child was screaming and blood from a cut on her forehead was mingling with the tears running down her little face.

"Here, Penny," said Mummy, "take care of this little girl while I go back to help her Mummy. Hold this clean hankie on the cut in her forehead and press hard, it's not deep. Try to comfort her." And, dumping the child down with Penny, Mummy ran back to the other car to help the others.

Penny went a bit pale when she saw the blood, but she was pleased and proud to be able to do something to help. She cuddled the frightened little girl who was only about four years old, and pressed the hankie on the cut forehead as Mummy had said.

Then she remembered the sweeties that she had, and managed to get hold of them and pop a nice red jube-jube into the little girl's mouth. This was a great help and the child soon stopped crying.

Then they saw Daddy helping the child's Mummy out of the car through one of the doors that he had forced open, though the car was still upside down. At the same time, Penny spied the African Nanny crawling out on her side of the car from underneath it. She did not seem to be hurt, though she looked quite dazed with the shock.

Then Mummy helped the other lady along to the Dawson's car, but she was limping badly and seemed to be in great pain.

But her chief thought was for her child.

"Joanie," she cried, "are you all right?"

How thankful she was to see her little girl sitting quietly now with Penny who had mopped up the blood from her face, and the bleeding had stopped.

Joanie's Mummy dropped down on the grass beside the car moaning, "My foot, my foot."

While Mummy attended to the poor woman's foot, Daddy was struggling to help Joanie's daddy to get out of the car. He had banged his head so hard on something that it had knocked him right out. Daddy managed to get him out at last and to lay him on the grass by the roadside.

Just then another car came up and stopped behind the Dawson's car and out jumped three young men and came up to see if they could help.

To the great relief of Mr. and Mrs. Dawson, one of the young men was a medical student, and he went to look at the driver who was unconscious.

The other two young men and Mr. Dawson now tried to turn the car the right way up, and Mummy said, "Billy, you can go and help them with the car."

Only too pleased, Billy ran off to help. Fortunately, it was not a very big heavy car, and between them they managed to get it right off the road, so that traffic could pass.

By this time the driver had come to and was sitting up,

though still suffering from shock. The medical student looked at the injured foot of Joanie's Mummy and said, "You ought to get into hospital with this foot, it will need to be X-rayed, Mrs.—"

"Judson is my name," said the lady.

"And my husband?" she asked, "is he all right?"

"He is a bit concussed, Mrs. Judson, but he doesn't seem to have any injury otherwise. You have all had a marvellous escape."

The African Nanny came up now and the little girl cried, "Nanny, Nanny," and held out her arms, and was taken by the African woman.

Daddy came up and after consultation it was agreed that the Dawson's would take Mrs. Judson and the little girl in their car and get them to the hospital in Salisbury as quickly as possible so that the injured foot could be dealt with.

The young men would bring Mr. Judson and the African woman in their car, and arrange for a garage to send out for the damaged car.

"By the way, how far are we now from Salisbury?" asked Daddy.

"Only about twelve miles or so, I should say," said one of the young men. Then he added, "I think I had better stay with the car till the break-down van comes, as all their stuff is in it."

"That would be very kind of you," said Mrs. Judson.

By this time her foot was so swollen and painful that the Dawsons decided to leave at once. They helped her on to the back seat of the car with her leg up across the seat, and the little girl and Penny sat with her, while Billy went into the front with Mummy, and away they went.

"I don't know what we should have done," said Mrs.

Judson, "if you good people hadn't come along just then to help us."

"I'm thankful that we were at hand," said Daddy, "you had passed us some way back."

"Yes, I'm afraid that we were hurrying more than we should have done," said Mrs. Judson, "we wanted to get home to Salisbury in time for a special party this evening. But," she added ruefully, "we shall not be there now, I'm afraid."

Soon the lights of Salisbury appeared in the distance, for by now it was dark.

"Could you direct us to the hospital?" asked Daddy. "We are strangers here and do not know Salisbury at all."

"Yes," said Mrs. Judson, "I will direct you, it's not far, we live here in Salisbury."

At long last they drew up at the Hospital, and Mummy and Daddy between them helped Mrs. Judson into the Casualty department.

While they were still there, the other car with the two young men and Mr. Judson arrived, and the medical student went in with him as he knew some of the staff there.

"Well," said Daddy to them, "you are in good hands now, so we will leave you, and I do hope you will soon be all right and suffer no serious ill-effects from your unfortunate accident."

"Thank you so very, very much," said Mr. and Mrs. Judson, "you have been real Good Samaritans to us."

As the Dawsons drove away to their hotel, Penny said, "That's twice our 'Silver Queen' has helped other people, isn't it, Daddy?"

"It certainly is," said Daddy, "she's living up to her name!"

CHAPTER VIII

SALISBURY AT LAST

"WELL," said Daddy, the next morning when they were having breakfast at the hotel, "here we are in Salisbury at last, our long, long journey over."

"Yes," said Mummy, "and we entered it in a quite unexpected way, making a wild dash for the Hospital."

"I wonder how poor little Joanie is this morning," said Penny.

"Daddy," cried Billy, "how many miles have we done all the way from London to here?"

"Well, now, son, you're asking something. Let me see —it was roughly six thousand miles from Southampton to Cape Town. Then from Cape Town the way we came by the Garden route—I shall have to work it out. Cape Town to Johannesburg was about sixteen hundred miles, and from Johannesburg here is just over seven hundred miles, but then we went round by the Game Reserve. I should say, son, that by our route we have done just over eight thousand, five hundred miles."

"Eight thousand!" exclaimed Penny, "what a long, long way!"

"Whew!" said Billy, "that's certainly *some* journey."

"Of course," said Daddy, "it would be a much shorter distance from London to Salisbury as the crow flies."

"But not being crows," said Billy, "we had to come round the long way."

"And now, here we are," said Mummy, "and I'm longing to go out and see the place."

"Well," said Daddy, "this morning, I must report to the office, but you and the children could go and have a look round the city, and we'll meet here at lunch-time."

Almost as soon as Mummy and the children left the hotel, Penny exclaimed:

"Oh look, Mummy, there's the black ladies selling lovely flowers like we saw in Cape Town."

Sure enough, they found that they were in Cecil Square, famous like Adderley Street for its flower-sellers.

After admiring the flowers, they wandered on into the city, looking at the very fine buildings and shops. At one place, at the junction of two wide streets, Billy recognised a statue of Cecil Rhodes.

"There's Rhodes again," he said, and really the children had begun to feel that he was quite an old friend of theirs, they had heard so much about him since they landed in Africa, and seen his picture or a statue of him in several places.

"I think Salisbury is a lovely little city," said Mummy, after they had wandered round quite a bit. "You know, children, don't you, that it is the capital?"

"The capital of Southern Rhodesia," said Billy.

"More than that," said Mummy, "it is now the capital city of the Federation, and that includes Northern Rhodesia and Nyasaland."

At lunch-time, Daddy came back to the hotel.

"Great news!" he said, when he saw them. "It seems that one of the men at the office and his family are going overseas for three or four months and we can live in their house while they are away."

"Wonderful!" said Mummy, "when can we go in?"

"In a week's time," said Daddy.

D

"That's lovely," said Mummy, "for I'm really getting tired of hotels now."

"And that will give us time to look for a house of our own, though they warn me at the office, that it's almost impossible to get a house here, and we may even have to build one. There are some fine new townships going up they say."

That afternoon, they all went to look at the lovely park for which Salisbury is famous. It was beautifully laid out and full of lovely flowers, and big shady trees.

"Oh, look Daddy," cried Penny, when they turned a corner, "there's a dear little waterfall."

They found that it was a lovely little model of the Victoria Falls and the Zambesi river which leads up to them. They spent quite a long time looking at this, and then went and had tea at the open-air restaurant.

"Well," said Daddy, "Salisbury can certainly be proud of Public Gardens like these."

On their way back to the hotel, they stopped to admire the floral clock in front of the Town House, and were intrigued to see that it actually worked.

"But how does it go, Daddy?" asked Penny.

"By electricity," replied Daddy. They watched this novelty for a while, and then it was time to go back to the hotel for supper.

"I must say," said Daddy, "that I like the look of the city where our new home is to be."

"So do I," said Mummy.

"So do I," echoed Penny.

"And the next thing to do," said Daddy, "is to see about schools for the children as soon as possible."

But Penny and Billy felt that there was no hurry for

this; they had enjoyed their long holiday tremendously and were not anxious to end it.

"Oh, yes," said Daddy, "the sooner you two are back to your lessons now, the better."

"I don't know how they are ever going to settle down again after all this excitement and travelling," laughed Mummy, "but once we are into a home of our own, we shall feel more settled."

The following week, the Dawson family moved into the home of the colleague who had gone overseas. It was a very nice house, and Penny and Billy and their Mummy and Daddy were very thankful to have the loan of it for three months.

The children ran all over it when they moved in, exploring the house and the garden.

"There's a lovely swing in the garden, Mummy," said Penny, "and lots of flowers."

"*And*," said Billy coming in at that moment, "there's a swimming pool too, what do you think about that?"

"You must be very careful, children," said Mummy, "not to make marks on this lovely furniture or on these beautiful carpets."

Once they were settled in their temporary home, Mummy and Daddy started house-hunting, but alas! they found that it was very difficult to get the right sort of house and in the right district near to the schools which the children would attend. They looked at the few that were available and decided that none of them would do. In the end they made up their minds to build a house in one of the new townships called Merridale.

After this, every evening Daddy pored over house plans. He drew some himself for he was a bit of an architect and he and Mummy had all sorts of ideas of what they would like to have in their new home, and even Penny and Billy had ideas on the subject too. It was to be a bungalow with no stairs.

One Saturday afternoon they went out to the township to choose the plot they wanted. That was very exciting. They looked at several, and finally decided on one that was on the side of a hill and from which they would have a nice view of the country. Meantime Penny and Billy started at their respective schools. Penny was delighted because the colours of her new school were two shades of blue with a band of gold between and she was thrilled when she went with Mummy to buy her school blazer.

She was very shy the first day that she went with Mummy to this new school, but in a few days she had settled down quite happily.

At last the plans for the new house were settled and passed, and one day, Daddy announced,

"They are going to start digging the foundations for our house to-day; on Saturday afternoon we must go out and see it."

So the next Saturday, they went out to inspect things where their house was being built.

Both Penny and Billy were amazed to see how deeply the builders had dug down for the foundations and what a strong concrete platform had been put down before the actual building could start. So Daddy explained how very, very important the foundation of a house was, and how the strength and safety of the house depended upon a good foundation.

The next time they went out, the walls had started to go up and some of the door-frames were in position. It was terribly exciting to Penny and Billy to watch their new home being built, and to pick out which would be their bedrooms. Penny's was to face east.

"So that the morning sun would come in and wake her up in the mornings," Mummy had said, for it must be admitted that Penny was a real little sleepy-head in the mornings.

There was to be a lovely big verandah right along one side of the house, and already in her mind's eye, Mummy could see lovely creepers like Golden Shower and Bougainvillia growing up the verandah posts, and moon flowers to fill the place with their fragrance in the evenings.

Mummy had wanted a thatched roof on the house, but because of the danger of fire if lightning struck it in the tropical storms, they decided to have a tiled roof, a rich red colour which went well with the reddy-brown bricks of which the walls were built.

"I think our house is going to be the nicest house in the whole world, Mummy," said Penny one day as they came away from visiting it.

"It will be nice, darling," said Mummy, "and if only it is finished in time for us to go into it when we have to leave the one we're in now, I shall be very thankful."

And it was.

CHAPTER IX

GOOD FOUNDATIONS

SOON after arriving in Salisbury, Penny's parents found out where the Baptist church was and started to go there to the Sunday Services. To their surprise the minister seemed to know all about them and gave them a specially warm welcome.

He was a dear old gentleman with silvery hair. He smiled at them and said,

"I knew you were coming, I had a letter from my friend in Cape Town, Mr. Green, telling me all about you, and I have been on the look-out for your arrival."

His name was Mr. Stevens, and Penny loved him as soon as she saw him. She and Billy went, of course, to the Sunday School.

"What a lot of Sunday Schools we've been to, Mummy," she said as they were setting out for the first time to this new one! "First there was our Sunday School at home in England that we always went to—then the one on the boat—then the one in Cape Town with Diane—then the Wayside one with the little black boys and girls—then the one in the Game Reserve—and now this one." Penny paused, quite out of breath with this long list.

"Yes," said Mummy, "but now you will be settled at this one for a long time, I hope."

On the Sunday morning after they had been out on the Saturday to see the foundations which had been laid for their new house, the Dawson family went to church as usual. It so happened that Mr. Stevens had chosen for his sermon that morning, the subject of the Parable which our Lord told of the two houses. First of all he read from St. Matthew. 8.

"Whosoever heareth these sayings of Mine and doeth them, I will liken him unto a wise man which built his house upon a rock.

"And the rain descended and the floods came, and the winds blew, and beat upon that house, and it fell not, for it was founded upon a rock.

"And everyone that heareth these sayings of Mine and doeth them not, shall be likened unto a foolish man which built his house upon the sand.

"And the rain descended, and the floods came, and the winds blew, and beat upon that house, and it fell, and great was the fall of it."

The old minister went on to explain this parable in simple terms for there were a lot of children in his congregation that morning. Vividly he described how the house built on the rock stood firm amidst all the buffeting of the storm. Rain, wind, storm—nothing could shake it from it's good strong foundation.

"That," he said, "is the position of the people who trust in Christ for their soul's salvation—who hear God's Word, and believe it, and obey it. The Lord Jesus Himself is called a 'Rock' in the Bible, it is upon Him that our hopes must rest. Our faith must be in Him, and in Him alone. If that is so, then when the storms of life come, the troubles and the testings, our faith will not fail, we shall stand firm like that house upon the rock.

"But those who hear God's Word, and do not believe and obey it, they are like the foolish man who built his house on the sand. They have no faith in God to keep them firm. When the storms come, down they go. These people put their trust in other things, not in the Lord Jesus, and when the testing time comes, these things let them down, they have nothing strong and firm to hold them.

"Oh, let us be wise to-day and put our trust in Jesus, the 'Rock of our salvation'! He will never fail the soul that trusts in Him, He will never let us down, and when the troubles and the storms come, we shall not be shaken, for He will uphold us with His mighty Hand.

"And now, for the sake of the little people here this morning let us sing the chorus about this.

"Build on the Rock, the Rock that ever stands,
O, build on the Rock, and not upon the sands;
You need not fear the storm, nor the earthquake shock,
You're safe for evermore if you build on the Rock."

Needless to say, Penny had listened with special interest to this little sermon and as it went on, she felt more and more excited. She longed to say, "We're building a new house and it's got very strong concrete underneath it, and our house won't fall down when the rain comes and the wind blows." But, of course, she had to keep all this in her heart till the Service was over. But as soon as she could, she ran over to the old minister and said,

"Our new house is ever so strong, it's got lots of cement and it isn't going to be built on the sand, so it won't fall down."

Mummy hastened to explain,

"Penny's specially interested in your sermon to-day because we are building a new house out at Merridale, and only yesterday we were out looking at the foundations for it which have been laid, and her Daddy was explaining why it must be made so strong underneath."

"Well, well," said Mr. Stevens, "so your house is built on concrete and won't fall down in a hurry! That's grand! And I wonder, Penny, if you understand what I was saying about putting our trust in Jesus, who is our 'Rock'?"

"Yes," said Penny shyly—"I—I trusted in Jesus on the boat when we came out from England."

"Good!" said the minister, "I'm so glad to hear that. May God bless you, my dear child!" As he spoke he laid his hand gently on Penny's fair, curly head, and somehow, it made her feel very happy, and—and good—as if she never wanted to be naughty again!

The chorus that the children had sung with great gusto was new to Penny, and later on when they were allowed to choose choruses in Sunday School, Penny chose that one until she knew it well. She loved the part where you give a tremendous clap with your hands as you sing, 'earthquake *shock*'! And whenever they went out to see the building now, Penny sang lustily as she ran round the new house,

"Build on the Rock, the Rock that ever stands."

It seemed to Penny and Billy that the day when the building of the house was finished would never come, but it did arrive at last. Then came the excitement of choosing and buying the furniture.

What a busy time Mummy had making the curtains and bedspreads! Penny was allowed to choose the material for her room. After spending a long time trying to make up her mind, she chose a pretty pattern of primrose flowers on a pastel blue background. Penny was delighted when she saw the lovely frilly bedspread on her new bed, and the curtains to match, and a pretty blue rug on the floor beside the bed. She could hardly wait for the day when they would move in to the new house.

Billy had chosen a fawn-coloured material with wild animals all over it for his room.

"Ough!" said Penny when she saw it, "I wouldn't like to sleep with those wild animals all around me, I should dream that they were chasing me."

At last everything was ready and the great day came when they moved into the new house. It was on a Saturday, so that Daddy could be home to help with the move. Penny and Billy did all sorts of little jobs to help Mummy too. It was all very exciting as they took possession of their new home.

It was a tired but very happy family that finally gathered round the supper-table that evening.

And when Mummy went in to tuck Penny up for the night, Penny said, "I've said my prayers, Mummy, and I've been saying 'Thank you', to Jesus for my own dear little blue bedroom."

"That's right, darling," said Mummy, "we are all very thankful for our nice new home, and I'm sure that we're going to be very happy in it. Sleep well now, and, 'Sweet dreams'!"

CHAPTER X

PENNY'S PARTY

"WE really ought to have a 'house-warming' party, I suppose," said Mummy one day soon after the Dawson family were settled in their new home, but we know so very few people here yet."

"And please let me get the garden a little more ship-shape before we have a party," begged Daddy.

There was a nice big garden around the house, or, rather, it was going to be a garden when Daddy and Elijah had finished laying it out.

Elijah was an African man who helped with the rough work and the garden. When Mummy first engaged him for the job, she asked if he had another name as she felt that it would be slightly—well—irreverent to be ordering Elijah to do jobs all over the place. She even suggested changing his name to something less Biblical, but he would not hear of it. Elijah was the name given to him at the mission-station up country where he had been born and he wasn't going to change it to please anybody! Behind his back, however, the family usually referred to him as 'the prophet'.

Anyway between them Daddy and Elijah had done wonders in turning the waste ground adjoining the house into the beginnings of a lovely garden. They had levelled lawns and planted them with grass, and dug and arranged flower-beds. They had planted a hedge of golden privet plants, and made a rockery outside the lounge windows.

According to his promise, too, Daddy was having not
only a swing, but also a see-saw put in, and later on he
planned to make a fish-pond with a little fountain in the
centre of it.

One great joy in the garden was a big old jacaranda tree
which was already in the ground when they bought it,
and which now graced one of the lawns and gave nice
shade for garden tea-parties. The neighbours told them
how lovely it would be in October when the tree would be
laden with delicate mauvy-blue flowers which, later on,
would drop and form a beautiful blue carpet below.

But to go back to the party. After further discussion,
it was finally decided that it would be best to wait and
combine the 'house-warming' party with Penny's birthday party in a month's time.

"Then," said Mummy, "the little girls in the neigh-
bourhood could come to Penny's party and their mothers
could come for the house-warming."

Yes, Penny was going to have a birthday when she
would be eight years old, and that day was drawing
excitingly near now. To her great joy, Mummy decided
to make a new frock for Penny for the party. It was to be
of white muslin with pale blue spots on it, with the skirt
very full and sticking out all round over a net slip as the
fashion was. Then a sash of the same blue as the spots
in the material would be a nice finish.

It *did* look lovely when Mummy had finished making it
and Penny could hardly wait for the day to come when she
would wear it. But that day came at long last. It was a
Saturday, and there was no difficulty about getting Penny
up that morning. She woke up very early and full of a
joyful feeling that something lovely was going to happen.
And indeed, all sorts of lovely things did happen that day.

The first excitement was Penny's birthday present from Mummy and Daddy which was a new small bicycle—the first she had had though she had had a tricycle and a scooter before.

How beautiful it looked with its shiny chromium parts! And how thrilled Penny was when she rode it up and down the gravel road in which they lived, to the great admiration of all the neighbouring children!

Billy gave her a new paint-box, a really super one which she had wanted for a long time.

Then when the postman came there were letters and birthday cards and one or two parcels from friends and relations in England. One that gave Penny a special thrill was a letter and pretty birthday card from Glenny, her friend up in Northern Rhodesia.

"But Mummy," said Penny, "however did Glenny know that it was my birthday to-day?"

"That's easy," said Mummy. "Don't you remember, one day on the boat coming out from England, when Glenny came round with a little red book which she called her birthday book, and she got us all to write our names in it on the date which was our birthday?"

"Oh, yes," said Penny, "I do remember that. Isn't it a pretty card, the flowers on it are forget-me-nots, that means we are never going to forget each other."

That morning Mummy had to go into town for some last-minute shopping for the party. When she came home, she called Penny and said:

"Who *do* you think I saw in town this morning?"

"Who, Mummy?"

"Mrs. Dennis—you remember the lady we met at the Zimbabwe Ruins, little Linda's mummy."

"Oh, Mummy!" said Penny, "and was Linda with her?"

"No," said Mummy, "Linda was at home; you see they live here, not very far away from us."

"Oh, I wish I could see dear little Linda again," said Penny.

"Well, your wish will soon be granted," said Mummy, "for I have asked Linda and her mummy to come to your party this afternoon."

"Oh, goody! goody!" exclaimed Penny dancing round joyfully.

After lunch Penny wasn't allowed to go into the dining-room where Mummy and a friend were busy setting the tea-tables, so she went out in the garden to sample the new swing and see-saw which Daddy had just managed to get fixed in time for the party. But soon it was time to go in and get dressed so as to be all ready before any of the guests arrived.

When she was dressed, Penny looked so lovely in her new party frock, with her golden curls all brushed and shining in the sunlight that Daddy decided he must take a colour picture of her right away.

Then the guests started coming, and Penny had a busy time greeting them and introducing them to each other. To her joy, little Linda remembered her at once and bestowed a dimpled beam on her as soon as she saw her.

It was a lovely afternoon and the children played out in the garden until Mummy called them in to tea. The dining-room doors were swung open, and in trooped all the little guests and were soon seated round the tables, little Linda being next to Penny. Before they began tea, they all sang,

> "*Happy birthday to you, Happy birthday to you,*
> *Happy birthday, dear Penny,*
> *Happy birthday to you.*"

Then they started on the lovely things that Mummy had prepared for the party, scones and pancakes, biscuits and fancy cakes, jellies and ice-cream, and in the place of honour, the big iced birthday cake which had Penny's name written on it in blue icing, and eight candles on it.

It was a very merry tea-party, and after it no-one felt like playing any energetic games. Also by now it was beginning to get dark, so the little guests crowded into the lounge, sitting all over the carpet, and Daddy showed them some films taken of the animals in the Game Reserve.

Just as these were finishing, there was a ring at the front door and in walked the old Baptist minister, Mr. Stevens. He had been invited to the party, but was not free to come till now. He had a great welcome, for everyone knew and loved him.

"Happy birthday, Penny," he said, and handed her a little packet. Penny opened it and when she found that it was a dear little blue birthday book, she was delighted.

"Oh, thank you so much," she said, "that's just what I wanted, a birthday book like Glenny's; now everyone must write their names in it."

After that Mummy played the piano and one of the older guests sang,

> *"Bless this house, O Lord I pray.*
> *Keep it safe by night and day."*

She sang it beautifully, and Penny thought the words were lovely, especially about the 'windows shining bright'. She looked up at the lounge windows which were open and the curtains had not been drawn. She could see the evening star twinkling away in the velvety darkness of the sky outside. It seemed to be twinkling specially at her as though to say, "I can see you, Penny, at your birthday party—happy birthday to you!"

By this time it was getting late for some of the tinies. Linda was already asleep with her curly head in Penny's lap, so her mother and others said they must go.

Then the old minister stood up and said,

"Before we go, let us bow our heads in prayer for a moment and ask God's blessing on this nice new house and on the big people and the little people who live in it."

In a few simple words, he prayed for God's blessing on this new home, and especially on Penny on her eighth birthday.

Then the 'Goodbyes' and the 'Thank you's' were said all round and the guests departed one by one till Mummy and Daddy and Penny and Billy were left alone.

"Well, my poppet," said Daddy, taking Penny on his knee, "has this been a happy day for you?"

"Oh, Daddy," said Penny snuggling down in his arms, "it's been the nicest birthday ever."

And later when Mummy was tucking up in bed a very sleepy Penny, she woke up enough to fling her arms round Mummy's neck and say,

"Thank you, Mummy, for a lovely, lovely party, and— and everything."

"And how does it feel to be eight?" asked Mummy.

"It feels nice," said Penny, and after a moment she added, "and now I'll soon be nine."

"Oh, don't grow up too quickly, little daughter," said Mummy.

"No, I won't," murmured Penny obligingly, and the next minute she was fast asleep.